STOV✓

Date Due

JUST SO STORIES SERIES

HOW THE RHINOCEROS GOT HIS SKIN

BY RUDYARD KIPLING

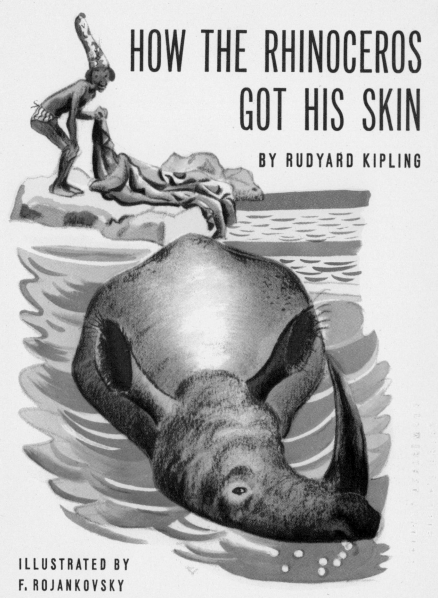

ILLUSTRATED BY
F. ROJANKOVSKY

GARDEN CITY PUBLISHING CO., INC., GARDEN CITY, N. Y.

Other Books in the
JUST SO STORIES *Series*

THE ELEPHANT'S CHILD
HOW THE CAMEL GOT HIS HUMP
HOW THE LEOPARD GOT HIS SPOTS

Printed in the United States of America
Designed and Produced by the Artists and Writers Guild, Inc.

HOW THE RHINOCEROS
GOT HIS SKIN

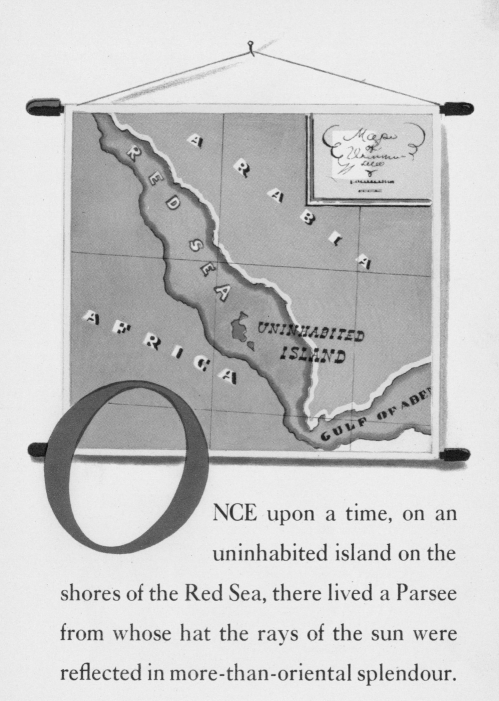

O NCE upon a time, on an uninhabited island on the shores of the Red Sea, there lived a Parsee from whose hat the rays of the sun were reflected in more-than-oriental splendour.

And the Parsee lived by the Red Sea with
nothing but his hat and his knife and a
cooking-stove of the kind that you must
particularly never touch. And one day he
took flour and water and currants and

plums and sugar and things, and made himself one cake which was two feet across and three feet thick. It was indeed

a Superior Comestible (*that's* magic), and he put it on the stove because *he* was allowed to cook on that stove, and he baked it and he baked it till it was all done brown and smelt most sentimental. But

just as he was going to eat it there came down to the beach from the Altogether Uninhabited Interior one Rhinoceros with a horn on his nose, two piggy eyes, and few manners. In those days the Rhinoceros's skin fitted him quite tight. There were no wrinkles in it anywhere. He looked ex-

actly like a Noah's Ark Rhinoceros, but of course much bigger. All the same, he had no manners then, and he has no manners now, and he never will have any manners. He said, 'How!' and the Parsee left that cake and climbed to the top of a palm tree

with nothing on but his hat, from which the
rays of the sun were always reflected in
more - than - oriental splendour. And the
Rhinoceros upset the oil-stove with his
nose, and the cake rolled on the sand, and

he spiked that cake on the horn of his nose, and he ate it, and he went away, waving his tail, to the desolate and Exclusively Uninhabited Interior which abuts on the islands of Mazanderan, Socotra, and the Promontories of the Larger Equinox. Then

the Parsee came down from his palm-tree
and put the stove on its legs and recited
the following *Sloka*, which, as you have
not heard, I will now proceed to relate:—

Them that takes cakes
Which the Parsee-man bakes
Makes dreadful mistakes.

And there was a great deal more in that than you would think.

Because, five weeks later, there was a heat-wave in the Red Sea, and everybody

took off all the clothes they had. The Parsee

took off his hat; but the Rhinoceros took

off his skin and carried it over his shoulder

as he came down to the beach to bathe. In

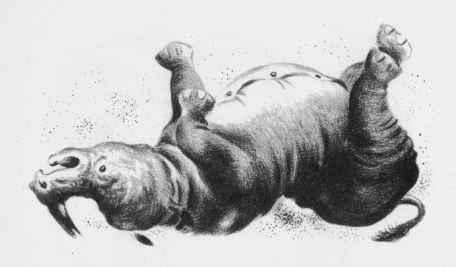

those days it buttoned underneath with three buttons and looked like a waterproof. He said nothing whatever about the Parsee's cake, because he had eaten it all; and he never had any manners, then, since, or henceforward. He waddled straight into the water and blew bubbles through his nose, leaving his skin on the beach.

Presently the Parsee came by and found
the skin, and he smiled one smile that ran
all round his face two times. Then he

danced three times round the skin and
rubbed his hands. Then he went to his

camp and filled his hat with cake-crumbs,

for the Parsee never ate anything but cake,

and never swept out his camp. He took

that skin, and he shook that skin, and he scrubbed that skin, and he rubbed that skin just as full of old, dry, stale, tickly cake-crumbs and some burned currants as ever it could *possibly* hold. Then he climbed

to the top of his palm-tree and waited for
the Rhinoceros to come out of the water
and put it on.

And the Rhinoceros did. He buttoned it up with the three buttons, and it tickled like cake-crumbs in bed. Then he wanted to scratch, but that made it worse; and then

he lay down on the sands and rolled and rolled and rolled, and every time he rolled the cake crumbs tickled him worse and worse and worse. Then he ran to the palm-

tree and rubbed and rubbed and rubbed
himself against it. He rubbed so much and
so hard that he rubbed his skin into a great
fold over his shoulders, and another fold

underneath, where the buttons used to be (but he rubbed the buttons off), and he rubbed some more folds over his legs. And it spoiled his temper, but it didn't make the least difference to the cake-crumbs. They were inside his skin and they tickled. So he went home, very angry indeed and horribly scratchy; and from that day to this every rhinoceros has great folds in his skin and a very bad temper, all on account of the cake-crumbs inside.

But the Parsee came down from his palm-tree, wearing his hat, from which the rays of the sun were reflected in more-than-oriental splendour, packed up his cooking-stove, and went away in the direction of Orotavo, Amygdala, the Upland Meadows of Anantarivo, and the Marshes of Sonaput.